SAM'S GIFT

SAM'S GIFT

ANN EDWARDS CANNON

SHADOW MOUNTAIN.

Library of Congress Cataloging-in-Publication Data

Cannon, A. E. (Ann Edwards)
    Sam's gift / by Ann Edwards Cannon.
        p.   cm.
    Summary: Sixth-grader Sam really misses Salt Lake City when he and his family move to New York, but a variety of experiences both in school and at home eventually help him adjust to his new surroundings.
    ISBN 1-57345-289-0 (pb)
    [1. Homesickness—Fiction.   2. Schools—Fiction.   3. Cats—Fiction.   4. Family life—New York (State)—Fiction.   5. New York (State)—Fiction.]   I. Title.
PZ7.C17135Sam   1997
[Fic]—dc21   97-36739
                                                                        CIP
                                                                        AC

Printed in the United States of America

10   9   8   7   6   5   4   3   2   1   8006

For Alec, who missed home

Thank you to all the students, teachers

and staff members at Tuxedo Park School

who made our year in New York

such a joyous experience

Prologue

We used to have a huge black cat named Shadow. He was already about a million years old when I was born, but he wasn't one of those grumpy cats that scratches little kids. In fact, we have pictures of me when I was a baby pretty much treating Shadow as if he were my personal pillow. I used to crawl all over him and put my head up right next to his, and he didn't even care. He'd just shut his eyes and purr and twitch his tail like a fly swatter. Mom said he acted like that because he liked me best of all. I was his *person,* she said.

A few days before we moved from Utah here to stupid New York, Shadow died because he was so old. Everything happened so fast I hardly had a chance to say good-bye. Not that I wanted to, anyway.

See, I really hate to say good-bye.

Chapter One

Oh no!

I can't believe this. I forgot to decide what I want to do for the Tuxedo Park School Sixth-Grade Holiday Talent Show.

It's bad enough that I forgot to do all those worksheets on insects last night. And also math. And also vocabulary, too. Now this.

Miss DiMarco—who looks like she should be somebody famous on TV, she's so pretty with her long black hair and eyes like a deer—is asking everybody what they want to do and then she's writing their answers down in a little notebook.

"I'm going to play the piano," Thomas tells her. I didn't know Thomas played the piano. He never mentioned that before.

Miss DiMarco smiles at him and then writes Thomas's answer down before asking Angela what she's going to do.

"I'm going to play 'Jingle Bells' on the flute."

"That will be very lovely, Angela. And what about you, Walker?"

"I'll do a piece on my violin," Walker says, licking his lips. "I haven't decided which yet."

Piano? Flute? Violin? I feel like I'm sitting in the middle of an orchestra. What will I say when it's my turn? I can't play an instrument. Or sing or draw either. I'm the Boy Without a Talent.

This is not good—not good at all. Next she'll ask Olympia, and then she'll ask Milo the Mosquito, and then she'll ask me. I wish I could say something that would totally impress her.

"What about you, Olympia?" Miss DiMarco asks. "What will you do for our talent show?"

Olympia stretches up real tall in her seat and then looks down her nose at everyone around her.

"I'm going to do a dance that I made up myself," she says in her I-Am-the-Queen voice. "It's about a little flower sleeping in the ground that comes to life in the spring. Naturally, I'm the flower."

I don't really mean to, but I groan out loud. Actually, I do think I mean to. Olympia is a royal pain. She'll tell you everything you don't want to know about her and more—that she has a tennis court and a swimming pool at her house, that she takes riding lessons, that her family has a live-in maid from Puerto Rico named Rosita. Miss

DiMarco gives me The Look—the one grown-ups use when they tell you to be quiet without actually moving their lips. I suddenly feel terrible.

"Milo?"

Milo the Mosquito is this brainiac kid who has a scholarship to Tuxedo Park School. He also happens to be totally annoying. For one thing, he knows everything about everything—especially math—which means he never shuts up in class. For another, he sounds like a machine gun when he laughs, besides which he always laughs in all the wrong places. Finally, he never *ever* combs his hair. You look at him sitting in front of you every morning reading his newest *Star Trek* novel, and you just want to say, "Hey, Milo! Go comb your hair!"

Milo shifts in his seat. "I don't know yet."

"I'll ask you again tomorrow, Milo." Miss DiMarco looks at me. "What about you, Sam?"

Here it is. The Moment of Doom. I, Sam Evans, cannot speak. Maybe she'll think I've got emergency laryngitis.

"Sam?"

"The oboe," I say. "I'm going to play the oboe."

The oboe? Now where did *that* come from?! I don't even know what one looks like! It's just a word I heard and remembered because I thought it sounded so funny. I sort of collect words that sound funny. Like *strudel* or *throat lozenges*. I like to say them real fast over and over. I don't even have to know what they mean. The only problem is that sometimes they fly right out of my mouth.

Words are always doing that to me—just leaving my mouth without my knowing it and getting me into very BIG trouble.

Miss DiMarco looks as happy as an announcer on a game show when one of the contestants gives the right answer. She smiles at me so much I almost turn red. "The oboe? I just *love* the oboe. My brother plays the oboe."

Oboe, oboe, oboe. I wonder if a person can learn how to play one by Christmas.

After school, while I'm waiting out front for my big brother, Ty, Milo the Mosquito is in my face just like—you guessed it—a mosquito. I don't know why, but he loves to bug me. He's a lot shorter than I am. Also skinnier. Doesn't he know I could squash him if I wanted to? Maybe he's not as smart as everybody says he is.

"You know what I think?" he's saying right now. "I think the Utah Jazz really stink."

Milo knows that the Utah Jazz is my favorite team. I even saw them play once in the Delta Center in Salt Lake City. It was the greatest. Dad took me—

just me—to watch the Jazz play the Knicks, whom I hate with all my heart. Dad kept saying he was sorry that our seats were so high up, but I didn't care. I loved being right there with the crowd, yelling and screaming and eating a bunch of junk.

The Jazz won 113 to 109.

That was before our family—Dad, Mom, Ty, our baby brother, William, and me—moved here to stupid New York, Land of the Knicks-Lovers.

"I watched them lose to Seattle on ESPN last night." Milo is going on and on like the most boring person you'd ever meet. I turn my back on him, and he laughs.

"Hey, Sammy boy." It's Ty, who's in the eighth grade this year. I'm not usually thrilled to see Ty. In fact, I keep a list in my head of all the reasons I am not usually thrilled to see Ty, which include the following:

1. He likes to steal my baseball hats and wear them.
2. He jumps into the front seat after I've called it and then locks all the doors.
3. He teases me about girls.
4. He pounds on me.
5. He plays his music too loud.
6. He gets straight A's in school, which makes

my parents think I ought to be getting straight A's in school, too.

7. He has friends in New York.

But at least Ty's presence at the moment causes Milo to buzz away. Ty's with his two best friends, Mason and Julio. The three of them like to get together and call girls on the telephone. They have these two girls they especially like—Paige and Virginia—whom they call Hairy and Scary.

I grunt hello. Julio and Mason smile. Mason wraps his arms around my neck and starts wrestling with me.

"Tell Mom I went home on Julio's bus, okay? I told her this morning, but she probably forgot already."

Ty is always saying stuff like that. He thinks he ought to be in charge of the world, he's so much smarter than the rest of us. I hate it when he babysits. We always have a fight about how to make the hot dogs. I like to cook mine in the microwave, whereas he says it's definitely better to fry them. Ty thinks he's the Hot Dog Expert just because he's two years older than I am. He thinks being two years older gives him the edge in the World of Hot Dogs.

"See you later, Sammy," Ty says as the bus rolls up.

"Later," Mason says, letting go of me. Julio plants a friendly slug on my arm. At least Ty's friends are pretty nice to me most of the time. A lot nicer than Ty, to tell you the truth.

The bus door swings open, and I watch the three of them climb aboard. I wish I were going to somebody's house to shoot hoops or play Sega. But instead I turn around and start to walk home alone, wondering what my friends in Utah are doing right this very minute.

We live about forty miles north and west of New York City. Early every morning before the sun is even up my dad takes the bus into midtown Manhattan where he works in a huge law office. Then he comes home after the sun sets. Some days I don't even see him. When we lived in Salt Lake City, Dad was only ten minutes away from his office. He used to fix us cereal every morning so Mom could go jogging with her buddies, Kathy and Sally and Nancy. Not seeing Dad is only one of the things I don't like about living here.

Also, I don't like going to a private school, although I have to admit that Miss DiMarco is probably about the best teacher I've ever had. She's really nice, and she knows how to turn schoolwork into games. Still, I wish Ty and I weren't in the same school again. If we were still in Salt Lake City, I'd be in the oldest grade at Wasatch Elementary, and Ty would be in his last year at Bryant Intermediate. Because Tuxedo Park School has grades K-8, however, I'm back to being the little brother again.

And here's another thing I don't like about going to a private school: they make you wear the same uniform every day—khaki pants, white shirt, green sweater. You can't even wear running shoes. You have to wear leather shoes like topsiders or loafers. How's a person supposed to run around at recess in those things?

Here's something good I discovered, though. One day at recess I saw a few of the older boys wearing baseball hats. I thought for sure they'd get in trouble, but none of the teachers cared as long as the kids took their hats off before going back to class. From then on, I started taking my best Jazz hat to school every day. It's the one Dad bought for me that night we went to the Delta Center together.

I decide to take a shortcut home through the trees. There are trees everywhere. When we first moved here, our parents kept pointing out how much fun we could have playing in all these trees.

"It looks just like Sherwood Forest!" Mom said about a million times. "You guys can be Robin Hood and his Merry Men."

Right. Like I'd want to go skipping through a bunch of trees wearing a pair of those stupid sissy ballerina pants.

Crunch. Crunch. Crunch.

The ground is covered with about a billion dry leaves. At first, when they were still hanging in the trees, they were bright red and yellow and orange. Even I thought it was pretty, although I for sure wouldn't let Mom or Dad know that. But now that the leaves have all dropped off and turned the color of old lunch bags beneath my feet, I think it feels even lonelier here than it did before.

It's the first week of December, and there isn't one bit of snow.

At home there's definitely snow. Grandma said so on the phone the other night when she called to talk to Mom. She said her old dog Thor was outside rolling around in it, making doggie angels. I'll bet my friends Nick and Ben and Mitch have already made runs for sledding at Lindsey Park. I'll bet they'll have snow for Christmas.

Christmas.

At home we get the same kind of tree every year—the big fat bushy kind. Do they even have trees like that in New York?

Crunch. Crunch. Crunch.

The branches of a bush just ahead move a little.

11

Something's hiding in there. Maybe it's a squirrel or a bird. Maybe it's a raccoon. We have a family of raccoons that live somewhere near our house. They go through our garbage cans every night, looking for snacks. Late one night Dad went outside, and a couple of raccoons sitting up in the branches pelted his head with empty soda cans and bread bags. Dad said they must not have liked the service at our place.

Crunch. Crunch.

Maybe this time there'll be a letter waiting for me in the mailbox when I get home. Maybe I can talk Mom into letting me call Nick tonight—

The bush moves again. I stop and hold my breath, waiting to see what's in it.

Suddenly, a humongous black cat pops out of the bush, and I nearly shoot out of my shoes.

The cat stops and gives me a good look. Then it blinks. I gasp. I've definitely seen this cat before.

"Shadow!" I say.

The cat turns and runs off, deep into the trees.

Mom's in the kitchen starting dinner when I get home. I don't even check the mailbox, because I can hardly wait to tell her about Shadow's twin. I toss my backpack onto the middle of the table.

Mom gives me a look that says she's (a) very

happy to see me and (b) if I don't clear my back-pack from the table, I will soon be toast. I groan, pick up the pack, and chuck it into the coat closet by the door.

"Thanks, I guess," Mom says.

I plop down in a chair.

"You sure burst through the door in a hurry," Mom says. "What's up?"

"I saw a cat in the woods that looks just like Shadow."

Mom smiles a little. "Old Shadow. I sure do miss him. I know you do, too, Sam."

I nod. I miss a lot of things, but right now I mostly miss Shadow.

"Are the Jazz playing tonight?" she asks after a little while.

"They played last night." I remember Milo so thoughtfully pointing out that fact.

"Have lots of homework?"

"Of course." I always have a lot of homework here. More homework than even Albert Einstein had. It's not fair the way they give you so much homework in New York.

Mom picks up a potato and starts peeling it.

"Ty went home with Julio," I finally remember to tell her.

"I'm sure he told you to remind me," she grins.

I grin back. "Where's Wills?"

"Taking a nap."

The kitchen is nice and warm, and even though we aren't having Tater Tots—which is what I personally would choose to have every night—whatever Mom's fixing smells pretty good. I like being alone with Mom. It's kind of hard to have a conversation with her when Ty and Wills are around. Ty talks all the time, and Wills moves all the time. He gets into the flour bin or pulls down soup cans or empties drawers. It's hard to get mad at him, though, because he's so cute.

"What did you do at school today?" Mom asks.

I shrug.

"Come on, Sam."

Yikes! I remember. The talent show! "Mom?"

She raises her eyebrows like question marks.

"Can we buy an oboe tomorrow?"

She practically drops that potato she's been peeling down the disposal. "An *oboe?*"

I nod.

"What in the world do you want with an oboe?"

"I want to—you know—play it, and stuff."

Mom laughs. "I can understand you wanting drums or an electric guitar. But an oboe?"

"Do you think I could learn to play it by Christmas?" I persist.

14

She just laughs some more. Usually I like the sound of Mom's laugh, even though she embarrasses Ty because she's so loud, especially in movie theaters. Right now, however, I don't think her laughing is a very good sign.

"Why do you want to play the oboe all of a sudden?"

I shrug again.

She narrows her eyes and looks at me closely. "Sammy?"

Maybe I should tell her about the stupid talent show. But then I'd have to tell her how I already told Miss DiMarco I'd play the oboe.

The phone rings, and Mom picks it up.

Yes! I'm off the hook!

"Hillary!" Mom smiles into the phone. "What a pleasure to hear from you! I just talked to your mother in Salt Lake, and she says you've enjoyed Colgate very much this year. I also told her we want you to spend Christmas with us, since you can't get off work long enough to fly home. And please invite anybody else who needs a place to stay . . . "

I sneak out of the kitchen, hoping she'll forget I ever used the word *oboe* in front of her.

Chapter Two

Miss DiMarco is talking to us.

"Before we start our rehearsal for the talent show, let me just say one thing. You are an amazingly gifted class. Every single person is either a musician or a dancer or an artist of some sort. This is incredible. I am so very proud of you!"

This is definitely not good. She's excited because she thinks I can play "Frosty the Snowman" on the oboe. Actually, I wish the oboe had never been invented. I hate the oboe. In fact, I am what you would call a true oboe hater.

And I don't even know what one looks like.

"All right, everybody," Miss DiMarco says, "please help me move your desks to the side of the room so that we have enough space to practice."

I groan as I stand up.

"The Jazz are gonna lose to the Knicks tonight! The Jazz are gonna lose to the Knicks tonight!"

Milo brushes past me, shoving his desk and singing an original composition.

It's been like this with Milo all day long. This morning before school started, he dropped an article from the *New York Times* on my desk that talked about how John Stockton always plays with his elbows up whenever he and the Jazz show up at Madison Square Garden. Naturally, I crumpled up the article into a meaningless little ball and banked it straight into the garbage can. Milo laughed and said, "Don't bother to thank me."

What is it with that guy? He's always saying snotty things about stuff I like. No doubt about it, Milo hates me, and I don't even know why.

Which is fine. I don't like him too much either.

When the last desk is moved out of the way, Miss DiMarco makes us sit in a semicircle on the floor.

"We'll just have a walk-through right now. That means you won't actually be performing. I'll call your name in the order you'll appear and then show you where to stand."

Whew! Now I won't have to use the line I've been practicing about accidentally leaving my oboe in Mom's car. I can save it for another time.

Anyway, we trot through the order of performance—I'm in the middle, just like at home—and then we put the room back together, after which

Miss DiMarco has us make invitations inviting our parents to come two weeks from today.

"Hey, Sam, really nice handwriting there," Miss DiMarco says, as she looks over my shoulder.

"Thanks," I say.

Too bad my invitation is going to wind up in the garbage can!

"So what would you think if I shaved my head?"

Ty and I are walking home from school together, and he's asking me how he'd look if he were bald.

I choose the right and tell him the truth. "I think you would look like a huge dork."

He snorts as if he doesn't believe me. Ty is one of those people who believes it isn't possible for him to look like a dork.

"See, I have this bet with Hairy and Scary. They bet me five dollars that I wouldn't shave my head."

Hairy and Scary live to make stupid bets with Ty.

"So if you don't shave your head, you lose five dollars, and if you do shave your head, you lose all your hair," I say.

Ty laughs as he kicks a rock and sends it flying. "It'll be funny. Everybody will love it when I show up tomorrow."

I shrug. Sometimes it's kind of hard having a brother be so happy in a place you really hate. Like New York, for example.

"Shortcut through the woods?" Ty asks.

He doesn't have to ask twice.

"Do you think it'll snow for Christmas?" I want to know as we go stomping through the leaves.

Ty scrunches up his eyes and stares straight up into the sky. "I hope so."

I really hope so, too. No snow for Christmas would be like no sugar on your breakfast cereal.

"It doesn't always snow for Christmas in Salt Lake," Dad said the other night when I told him my whole Christmas would be totally ruined if there wasn't any snow.

"But everything else is the same there," I told him. Same kind of tree with the same ornaments in the same house with the same friends to call on Christmas morning so you can see if they got the same kind of stuff you got. Besides, I think Dad is wrong. There is too snow for Christmas in Salt Lake. Always.

"Wow!" says Ty, pointing at the branch of a tree just ahead. "Look at the size of that cat!"

It's Shadow again, sitting there on the branch just like the Cheshire Cat in *Alice in Wonderland*.

"He looks just like Shadow used to," Ty breathes.

Swallowing hard, I nod.

"I wonder who he belongs to," Ty says.

"I think maybe he's lost."

"Do you think we ought to take him home?"

I would like that. I would like that very much. I nod.

"Here, kitty kitty kitty," Ty starts yelling at the top of his lungs. The cat freezes and goes all stiff.

"Shhh," I say. "You're scaring him."

But Ty keeps right on yelling.

"Ty," I whisper loudly, "be quiet!"

Ty starts running toward the tree. The cat streaks down the trunk and scampers off into the woods. Normally I would be mad at Ty, whose face has just crumpled in disappointment.

But here's the thing: that cat looked straight at me—*me*—before he took off. It was as if he was saying that maybe the two of us could be friends someday.

Mom's on the phone when we get home. Again.

"Yes," I hear her say, "we'd love to have you both come for Christmas! The boys will be so excited! They're just coming through the door now."

"Who was that?" Ty asks as soon as Mom hangs up.

"You're never going to believe it, but guess who's coming for Christmas!"

"Santa Claus?" Ty asks. He thinks he's such a comedian.

Mom smiles and brushes his answer away. Then she gives us the real one. "Aunt Shirley and Aunt Joyce!"

Aunt Shirley and Aunt Joyce aren't really our regular aunts. They're great-aunts. Maybe even great-great-aunts. Something like that. I think they're both pretty close to eighty years old.

"It's amazing, isn't it," Mom is saying, "that two women their age still get out and do things! They just said they haven't been to New York City since World War II, and they want to see it at least one more time." Mom shakes her head. "I hope I'm just like them when I'm their age."

Aunt Shirley and Aunt Joyce are okay. Better than okay, in fact. They're the only adults I know who will sit down and play an entire game of Monopoly with you even if it takes three hours. Also, they always give you popcorn balls and bags of candy.

"*YES!*" says Ty. "I love it when Aunt Joyce and Aunt Shirley show up."

"What about you, Sam?" Mom asks. "Aren't you happy that they'll be here with us for Christmas?"

"Sure," I say. It's just that I'd rather spend Christmas with them in Salt Lake. This is something I get ready to point out to Mom, but she's already busy saying something else.

"Let's see now," Mom starts counting on her fingers, "that makes three guests for Christmas so far."

"Hey, Mom, do you think Dad will let me shave all my hair off tonight?" Ty wants to know.

Mom blinks a few times and then laughs. "When your father was your age, he was trying to figure out how to let his hair grow down over his collar before Grandpa trotted him off to the barbershop."

"Can I, Mom? Can I? Can I?"

Neither one of them notices me slipping away as quietly as the big black cat in the woods.

Chapter Three

I'm standing by myself in front of a group of people, holding some sort of strange instrument, getting ready to play it. Only I don't know how to play it. Maybe it's an oboe. But then how would I know?

My hands are sweating. My knees are knocking against each other. I think I might accidentally throw up on everybody in the audience just as Timmy Billings did that day in reading group when we were in the first grade. Even now, whenever I think about Timmy Billings, I remember how he turned as white as chalk and then started hurling on us all. Some of the girls even had to call their mothers and ask them to bring clean clothes. That'll be me. From now on when anybody in the entire state of New York sees me, they'll say, Remember the talent show and how Sam Evans threw up all over the first row?

"Sam? Sammy?"

I pop open one eyelid. I notice I'm still in bed and I'm not actually holding an oboe. Also, there's nobody standing around looking worried that I might throw up on them. So far, so good.

"Wake up, sleepyhead. I'm starting pancakes," says Dad, poking his head into my bedroom.

Yes! It's Saturday morning. Dad always makes pancakes for us on Saturday mornings. It's the only time we get to see him these days.

"Hurry and get dressed. I'm taking requests in five minutes," he says.

Dad does requests like those radio guys on the country-western station do. You know what I mean: "This next Garth Brooks song is for Betty Jean from her ever-lovin' man, Dan." Stuff like that. (For the record, I do not listen to country-western unless I am forced to, such as when my father is driving the car and gets to control all the buttons.)

Anyway, Dad does requests for pancake shapes—Mickey Mouse, Big Bird, dinosaurs, flowers. You get the idea. All the pancakes end up looking exactly the same, but Dad tries hard, anyway.

I jump out of bed and run straight to my window, just as I always do before putting on my clothes. I want to see if it snowed last night, although I don't think it did. You know how sometimes you can tell it's snowed even before you look outside because the light in your room is kind of different? Well, it wasn't different when I opened my eyes after the oboe nightmare. Still, I hope a little.

I pull the drapes open, and—I'm right again. No snow some more.

I think about all my friends back home. Since it's Saturday, Nick and Ben and Mitch will be up at Lindsey Park today with their saucers and tubes, blasting down the hill and catching air while I'm stuck here in stupid, nonsnowing New York.

Maybe they've forgotten me already. Can friends do that? I haven't received a letter for a long time.

I've known Mitch and Ben and Nick since kindergarten. Mom called us the Four Musketeers because we were always doing stuff together—playing over the line, going to movies, shooting rounds at the University of Utah golf course. Even when we weren't really doing things, we were together, just hanging out. I never needed any other friends.

And then we moved here.

Ty, of course, found Mason and Julio right away. Me, I don't know what to say to the kids in my class. Not that I really want to, anyway. Besides, I'd probably just look stupid if I did.

When I get dressed, I put on every single Utah Jazz thing I own—shorts, shirt, sweatshirt, and hat. I look at myself in the mirror with all my Utah Jazz stuff on, and suddenly I start to feel a little sick inside.

By the time I get to the kitchen, in fact, I feel pretty rotten, even though it's Saturday and Dad's standing over the griddle wearing his Cubs baseball cap backwards. Thank goodness he hasn't turned into a Yankees lover, although I'm sort of surprised he hasn't, since everybody in this family seems to love it here so much. Everybody except you-know-who.

Mom's strapping Wills into his high chair. "Hi, Sam." She doesn't really look at me, so she can't see all my Jazz clothes.

Ty's at the table. "Hey, Dad. I want you to do something really hard. It'll be a stretch for you. Okay? I want you to do—AN AMOEBA!" Then he bursts into laughter like he's such a funny guy. I punch him when I walk past.

"Ouch! That hurt!" he yells, but he doesn't go after me, which means he must be in a pretty good mood. Hopefully, I can change that. Hopefully, I can make him and everyone else feel as miserable as I do.

"Honestly, Sam, what was that all about?" Mom turns around to look at me. Finally. She pauses a little and then asks, "Shorts in December?"

"Who cares?" I grumble. "There's no snow out there."

I see Mom and Dad look at each other. They've been doing that a lot lately after I say stuff. In fact, I find myself saying stuff just so they will exchange one of those looks.

"So, Mr.-Wear-Your-Shorts-in-December," Dad says as if nothing is wrong, "what do you want me to make you?"

I shrug.

"I'm making a tennis racket for Mom, a bottle for the baby, and an amoeba for Ty."

"And it will be amazing how much they all look exactly like pancakes," Mom cracks. Dad pulls a face at her.

"So what will it be, Sam-I-Am," Dad says again.

"Utah," I say slowly. "Make me the state of Utah. Make the Great Salt Lake. Then make me the mountains, and cover them with snow. Tons and tons of snow. Okay?"

Nobody says a word until Ty opens his mouth. "Duh, Sam."

This time I really let him have it. He lets me have it back.

"BOYS!" It's Mom, and she isn't happy. "You both need to cool down. To your rooms. Now!"

Ty gives me a little shove in the back as we go up the stairs. "Thanks a lot, loser," he says.

When I get upstairs I go to the window and just stare out of it—stare and stare and stare some more at the trees across the street.

Wait a minute—

I think I see it again. Maybe it's one of the crows that hang out here. Right color. Right size. But no! There he is again.

Shadow.

He's across the street, and he's staring straight up into the window—*my* window. In fact, he's staring straight up at *me!*

Don't go! I tell him in my mind. *I'll be there as soon as I can. This time there won't be anyone crashing through the trees, chasing you and scaring you off, because this time I'm not bringing Ty along. It'll just be you and me.*

I sneak out of my bedroom so Ty can't hear me, take the front staircase down, and slip out the door without anybody in the kitchen seeing me, but it's already too late. By the time I cross the street into the woods, Shadow isn't there.

He's pure gone.

I'm so disappointed I can taste it. I really thought he was going to wait for me, be there when I came for him.

I go poking around a little bit, looking for him, calling him softly—unlike a certain person who scares cats away every time he opens his very large mouth.

No cat anywhere.

Not under trees or shrubs or behind logs or rocks.

"Please!" I say out loud.

Then suddenly I remember something I read in a book once—or at least I think I read it—that some people have this special power to talk to animals in their heads. I'm pretty sure I'm not making this up. Anyway, I think I could be one of those people.

I sit down on a tree stump and close my eyes so I can really concentrate.

Come here, Shadow. I'm your buddy, your pal. Come to me.

I pop one eye open and then close it. No cat. So far.

I promise you'll love my house. We've got soft pillows to sleep on. Bowls of vanilla ice cream everywhere. Mice in the basement. It's Cat Heaven.

I keep my eyes closed, but I listen hard, hoping I'll hear Shadow the way you sometimes do with animals. You'll hear them rustling around in the lilac bushes by your front porch long before you ever see them.

I keep concentrating and concentrating until my eyes hurt from keeping them shut so hard.

"Sam! Sa-a-a-a-m!" It's Mom calling for me from the porch. I guess they figured out I'm not in my room anymore.

"SAM!" Dad's walking down the driveway, towards the trees. Time's running out.

I open my eyes now and start calling out loud in a low, friendly voice. "Shadow!"

"Sam? Is that you, Sam?" Dad answers.

"Shadow! Come here, boy."

"Sam, I want to talk to you—" Dad's getting closer.

"You've got to hurry, Shadow. They're gonna make me go inside and talk!"

I guess that does the trick, because suddenly Shadow is right in front of me, just sitting at my feet. I reach down to pet him, wondering if he'll let me pick him up.

I stoop down—easy does it—and lift Shadow into my arms. He doesn't fight me one bit.

"Sam—" Dad suddenly appears through the trees. When he catches sight of Shadow and me, his mouth pops open. Mom's reaction is pretty much the same a few minutes later when she sees Dad and me walking up the driveway, Shadow tucked in my arms, feeling as heavy as a huge load of laundry.

"Where on earth—" she starts to say.

"This is the cat I was telling you about, Mom. He looks just like Shadow, doesn't he?"

She's speechless.

"He weighs about as much as Shadow did, too," I add.

Mom and Dad look at each other.

"Anyway," I keep right on talking, "I really think we ought to keep him. I'm pretty sure somebody moved away and couldn't take him."

Dad scratches Shadow underneath his chin. Shadow stretches out his neck, just to make sure Dad hits all the right spots.

"I don't know, Sammy," he finally says. "This guy looks pretty well fed to me. He looks like somebody's pet."

I hold Shadow just a little tighter against my chest. "Then why's he been hanging out in the woods?"

"Maybe he's lost, sweetheart," Mom says.

"I don't think so," I tell her.

Mom strokes Shadow's fur. "He really looks just like old Shadow, doesn't he?"

She's softening. This is good. Very good.

"Can he stay with us?" I ask.

31

"What about it?" Mom asks Dad.

Dad clears his throat. "I think if this were our Shadow and he got lost, we would appreciate it very much if somebody tried to find us. Don't you?"

I don't answer, but Mom says Dad's right. Of course.

"I'll tell you what," Dad goes on. "I'll run an ad in the paper and put a few fliers around town—at the train station, bus stop, police station, IGA—and if nobody claims him in a week, we'll keep him. All right, Sam?"

"*Yes!*"

Here's the thing. Nobody's going to claim Shadow. I just know it.

I'll tell you something else—finding this cat has been the *best* thing that has happened to me since I moved to New York.

Chapter Four

Isn't it funny how you can have practically the best day of your life followed by one of the worst ever?

That's what's happening to me. It's Monday afternoon, and I'm sitting outside the headmistress's office while Sheila the Secretary is calling my mom because I am in BIG TROUBLE.

Before I tell you about that, though, I want to back up to Saturday just so you can see how horrible my life is right now compared to what it was like only two days ago.

You already know about the first good thing—that Shadow moved in with us. At first Ty said we needed a different name because using the same name over again was (a) boring and (b) stupid. So Mom gave everybody a pen and some paper and made us write down all the names we could think of.

These were Ty's names:
1. Killer
2. Mouse
3. Killer Mouse

These were Dad's names:
1. Frank Chance
2. Joe Tinker
3. Johnny Evers

Now here's Mom's list:
1. Sylvester
2. Garfield
3. She says she has no imagination

Even Wills had a list, which Mom made up for him:
1. Blacky
2. Midnighty
3. Velvety

But in the end, all of us, including Ty, agreed that Shadow was the best name of all. So we named him Shadow's Shadow—Shadow for short—and he has been acting as if he owns the place ever since. He jumps up on the kitchen counter and sits on all the furniture whenever he feels like it, even when

Dad tells him to get off. Shadow's very favorite spot, though, is my bed.

So that was the first good thing about Saturday.

Later, we all piled into the car and went to this farmer's market in New Windsor where we found a big fat tree that looks a lot like the ones we always bought in Salt Lake.

Not quite as good, maybe, but almost.

We didn't even have to fight about which tree we wanted. When we saw it, we knew it was the one for us—even Ty agreed. So Mom wrote out a check, and Dad and one of the guys who worked at the farmer's market tied the tree to the top of the car.

Then we took it home and put it up in the living room. The minute we dragged it inside, the whole house smelled like Christmas tree—the best smell in the universe.

Dad and I went up into the attic and found our boxes full of lights and ornaments. First, Mom wrapped the lights around the tree, grumbling the whole time about lazy fathers and sons. Then we started hanging the ornaments: the fake red apples and the felt angels Grandma made us, the ornaments with our birthdays on them and the ones Ty and I made in school, the ornaments from our trips to places like Bryce Canyon and Disneyland. The oldest ornament we have is one that used to be on

35

Dad's tree when he was a little boy. It's an elf sitting in a silver chair. Dad said he used to love looking at it when he was little, so Grandma Evans gave it to him the first Christmas he and Mom were married.

Even Shadow got into the spirit of things. He was chasing one of the satin balls around the floor, smacking it with one of his paws just as if he were playing hockey. Also, he kept trying to snag the fake red birds Mom hung on the tree. She managed to keep most of them safe, but I noticed Shadow had feathers in his mouth once or twice.

By the time the tree was all decorated, it was dark outside, so Dad plugged in the Christmas tree lights and put on a Bing Crosby Christmas CD while Mom served up mugs of hot cocoa with candy canes for stirring. Then we all closed our eyes while Bing Crosby was singing "White Christmas" and pretended there was a ton of snow outside.

For just a minute while we were all sitting in front of the tree, watching it shine, listening to the music, and sipping our cocoa with the melting candy canes, I thought maybe—just maybe—Christmas in New York might not be so bad after all.

And then came today. Monday. Monday and Milo. Milo the Mosquito.

"The line is still busy," says Sheila the Secretary

to me as she puts down the phone for the third time and brings me straight back to the present.

"Oh," I say and then look out the window at millions of bare, brown, unsnow-filled trees.

"I'll wait another five minutes, and then I'll call her again. You stay where you are." Even though I'm not looking at her, I can tell she's giving me the version of The Look that nails you to whatever chair you happen to be sitting in.

So let me tell you about Milo.

He started early with me today. First thing this morning, before the bell even rang, he was at my desk trying to grab my notebook. Very annoying. Later, during class, whenever he caught my eye, he started mouthing some words to me. I finally figured out that he was saying "THE JAZZ STINK." But the big problem occurred during recess after lunch.

Remember how I told you about my little discovery—that you could wear a baseball cap during recess and the teachers wouldn't bug you about it? And remember how I told you about my Jazz hat that Dad bought for me at the Delta Center? Well, I wore it today. I put it on as soon as lunch was over and went outside to kick a soccer ball around. That's when Milo showed up and started bugging me some more. The next thing I knew, he grabbed my hat and took off with it.

I screamed at him, but he just kept running and laughing like a stupid hyena. So I ran after him.

As soon as I almost caught up with him, he chucked my hat straight into a dirty puddle.

Well, I just went nuts after that. I snagged Milo, picked him up, and threw him into that puddle, too, so that his pants and sweater were splattered— just like my favorite hat. Milo looked up at me with this shocked look on his face.

And then he started to cry.

"Sam Evans!" It was Mrs. Dizengoff, the teacher on recess patrol. She was stomping toward me like ten armies rolled into one person. Kids stopped what they were doing to watch. I didn't even care that they were all staring at me, even though normally I would hate that. I was still so mad I was shaking.

"What is going on here!" Mrs. Dizengoff snagged my arm.

I didn't say anything.

"He shoved me!" Milo yelped.

"Because you took my hat, you stinking little freak!" I shouted straight at him.

"That's enough," Mrs. D. barked. "Both of you.

I think Miss Baylor will want to see you in her office."

Which of course she did. The two of us—me and Milo in his totally dirty uniform—sat in front of her desk while she chewed us out in her fancy English accent. Basically I just stared at my feet. Sometimes I accidentally stared at Milo's feet, although I tried very hard not to.

Anyway, she decided that as part of our punishment we had to call our parents and tell them what had happened. Milo went first. He called his dad, who was at work, and told him I had thrown him into a ten-foot hole full of mud. When Miss Baylor cleared her throat, he added the part about how he'd thrown my hat in the mud, too, and that maybe he'd even thrown it in there first.

Then it was my turn. I was shaking when I picked up the phone, although I tried very hard not to look nervous in front of the Mosquito. The line was busy. It stayed busy, too.

"Maybe the baby took the phone off the hook," I said. "Sometimes he does that." Wills loves the telephone. Once back in Salt Lake City he even dialed 911 by accident, which caused the police to show up at our house for a little chat.

Finally Miss Baylor excused Milo but told me to

39

stay behind, which is why I'm sitting in the reception area with Sheila the Secretary.

Sheila the S. picks up the phone again, puts it up to her ear, and dials.

"At last," she tells me. "Mrs. Evans? This is Sheila Romanski from the school, calling in behalf of Miss Baylor. I have Sam here with me. He's been asked to tell you something."

Sheila the S. hands me the phone.

"Hi," I say, using my ill voice. Maybe if she thinks I have some sort of rare disease she won't get mad at me.

"Are you all right?" Mom asks.

I shrug.

"What's going on, Sammy?" She sounds impatient, which is not a great sign.

"Well," I begin, "I had a little trouble at recess."

"What kind of trouble?"

"You know Milo? The kid who keeps torturing me at school? Well, he took my hat—the special Jazz one that Dad bought me—and he threw it in the mud."

"And—"

"So I sort of threw Milo in after it."

Mom explodes. "Sam Evans! What in the world is going on inside that beautiful, unhappy head of yours?!" Her words practically leap out of the telephone at me. "I'm having a horrible day. The worst ever! The bottom of the grocery bag ripped out, and a huge jar of mayo broke all over the driveway. Wills raced ahead of me into the house and then proceeded to lock me out for twenty minutes. And now my washing machine is overflowing, and I've been on the phone trying to find just one human being on the east coast who can be bothered to come fix it sometime before the end of the year. The absolute last thing I need right now is a sulky sixth grader. I'll deal with you later, Sam Evans. Let me talk to Mrs. Romanski again."

I hand the phone back to Sheila the S., who looks as if she feels a little sorry for me, even though she's not supposed to. "Yes, Mrs. Evans, I'll let Miss Baylor know you've spoken with Sam."

Sheila the S. hangs up the phone. "Back to class with you, mister." Only when she says *mister*, it sounds like *mistah*.

When I go back to class, I try to ooze around the sides of the room so that no one will notice me, but it doesn't work. Everyone looks up from their response journals and watches me. Everyone except Milo, even though I'm pretty sure he knows I'm in the same room with him. He just keeps scribbling away, although I do notice that two bright red spots are burning in the middle of his cheeks.

41

Miss DiMarco nods at me without smiling when I slide into my seat. My stomach does a little flip. I think I've disappointed her.

I take my journal out of my desk, pretend to be busy, and don't look up until it's time for afternoon recess. Naturally, the Mosquito and I don't get to go out. We have to stay inside and talk to Miss DiMarco, who's gotten the details of our fight from Mrs. Dizengoff.

"We need to talk," Miss DiMarco says. "You two clearly have a problem with each other, and we need to work something out. Don't you agree?"

At this point Miss DiMarco gives us both a little smile, so I grunt just to show her that I'm listening. Milo, on the other hand, does not grunt. In fact, he says nothing at all.

"Let's start with you, Sam. Clearly, it is not acceptable for you to use physical force when settling an argument. What could you have done differently?"

I want to say that I'd do the same thing over again only this time I'd wash his face with mud while I was at it, but I don't think that's exactly the answer she's looking for.

"What about it, Sam?"

"I guess I could tell him to please give my hat back." Right. Like he would. But this answer makes

42

Miss DiMarco pretty happy, and she gives me one of her better smiles.

"And you, Milo, what could you do to become a better friend to Sam?" She gives him a smile, too, although anybody can see it's not as good as the one she just gave me.

Milo doesn't say anything. He's so rude.

"Milo?"

Milo looks at Miss DiMarco, at me, and then at Miss DiMarco again. "I thought we were already friends. At least I did until today."

Friends? Me and Milo? I am definitely in shock. Miss DiMarco looks surprised herself.

His cheeks get all red again, just as they did when I walked back into the room from the secretary's office, and for one pretty horrible minute I think he's going to start crying again.

But he doesn't. He just swallows hard and says, "May I be excused now?"

Miss DiMarco almost says something but ends up nodding instead. Milo gets up quietly and leaves the room without looking back.

After he's gone, Miss DiMarco turns to me. "So what do you think about that, Sam?"

"I don't know."

Miss DiMarco looks after Milo thoughtfully. "I don't know what I think, either. Tell me when you have an idea, okay? Outside you go, Sam. No more fights. We can't risk any injuries to those musical fingers of yours before the talent show. Right? We'll have a practice during the last hour of school today."

Great. First Milo and now this—another practice. I forgot again. What am I going to tell her this time?

"Uh, Miss DiMarco?"

"Yes?"

"I couldn't bring my oboe today."

She raises her eyebrows.

"It's in the shop!" I blurt out the first thing that comes into my head. Dad is always saying our car is in the shop, so why not an oboe? "It's being fixed."

"Well," Miss DiMarco takes a deep breath, "just as long as you're ready for the talent show."

"I will be," I promise her. "I will!"

As I walk through the kitchen door after school, I can't help but wonder what Mom's going to say about my little problem with Milo. No doubt about it, she sounded pretty upset when I called her from the school this afternoon.

But when I walk through the door—surprise!—she's on the telephone. I hold my breath, hoping that it's not somebody calling about Shadow.

"Oh, please do, Hillary," she says. "We'll have so much fun! And please tell your mom hi for me when you speak again." Mom says good-bye and hangs up. "Hillary's definitely spending Christmas with us, and she's bringing one of her roommates, so now we'll be having four guests for Christmas."

Mom looks at me as if she's just realized I'm in the same room with her. "Hey there, Sammy."

Well, so far she doesn't sound as if she's going to make me miss dessert for the rest of my life.

"Hey there, Mom. Where's Shadow? I better go check on him."

Mom puts her hand on my shoulder and gives me a little smile. "Shadow's fine. The last time I saw him, he was curled up on your pillow. Okay? So pull up a chair and let's talk about today, now that I've cooled down."

Here we go again. Everybody wants me to tell them about today, which I do, but when I get to the part about Milo saying he thought we were friends, I stop.

"What's the matter, Sam? What did Milo say?"

I shake my head.

How can I explain this? I hate Milo. I hate Milo so much, in fact, I wish he had to wear a dress to school for the rest of the year as a punishment. But I keep thinking about the way he looked as if he wanted to cry but wouldn't and then how he walked out of the room alone so quiet. Thinking about it makes me feel strange somehow.

It makes me feel . . . sad.

Chapter Five

Okay, this is going to be one of those super short chapters that kids who have to write book reports especially like. I just wanted to tell you about something really terrific that happened earlier tonight.

It's been nearly a week since Shadow came to live with us. During that time he's become a true member of the family. I know as much about him as I know about my brother Ty. You can even see this for yourself with the following lists of favorite things:

	TY	SHADOW
Favorite food	pizza	Tender Vittles
Favorite place to snooze	his bed	my bed
Favorite sport	baseball	pouncing on feet
Favorite comic strip	Calvin & Hobbes	Garfield
Favorite place to be scratched	? ? ? ? ?	under his chin

Come to think of it, I actually know *more* about Shadow than I do about Ty, as these lists demonstrate.

Anyway, when Dad came home from work tonight—Ty and I were still up because it's Friday—he said he was taking us all into Manhattan tomorrow to see the Christmas displays. Naturally we all jumped up and down and gave Dad high fives and made a bunch of noise that scared Shadow so much he shot off the couch, leaped over Dad's shoes, and scampered straight up the stairs.

Dad laughed. "I never thought such a huge cat could move so fast!"

"Dad?"

He looked at me.

"You remember all those posters and stuff you put up around town?"

Dad nodded.

"Well, nobody's called."

"Is that a fact?"

"Can Shadow stay, Dad? Please?"

Dad pressed his lips together tight, as he always does when he's thinking hard. "I think so, Sammy. I think so."

So that's it. My short chapter. Shadow officially belongs to us. Now I won't have to jump every time the phone rings!

Chapter Six

"But it'll cost five times as much." This is Dad talking to Mom.

"I'd just be a lot more comfortable taking cabs today instead of trains, okay?" This is Mom speaking to Dad. "Especially with a baby. Especially on a weekend. You yourself always say the subway is a different place on the weekends."

Dad groans because Mom has obviously scored a direct hit.

They're having one of those conversations where you, the kid, are not supposed to be listening. It's Saturday. The five of us are driving into Manhattan to see all the Christmas stuff there, and Mom and Dad are having a fight about whether or not we're going to use the subway today. Ty's the one who brought it up. He loves the subway.

"Please, Mom," says Ty.

"No. Nein. Nicht. How many more languages do I need to use here?" Mom says.

Ty snorts and sinks back into his seat. You can tell from his face that he's decided already that his whole day has been ruined. Dad looks put out, too, which makes me feel kind of sorry for Mom. I think she's a little afraid, even though she's not usually the kind of mom who's afraid of things. When we went to Disneyland, for example, she was the one who went on Space Mountain with me, whereas Dad was the one who volunteered to sit out with Wills. It's just that she doesn't go into the City every day the way Dad does.

"Come on, you guys," Mom says, "let's not ruin our Christmas spirit here." She opens up the glove compartment and rustles around in it until she pulls out a Christmas CD. Bing Crosby. The same one we listened to when we were decorating the tree. We have other Christmas CDs, but Mom always plays this one. She says it reminds her of being a little girl all over again.

We pull up to a tollbooth to pay to cross the George Washington Bridge into New York City just as Bing starts to sing my favorite song, "Little Drummer Boy." I sing along.

"'Come, they call me—'"

"You sing like a girl," says Ty.

"Big deal. You look like a girl!" Then I add a few

rum-pum-pum-pums to catch up with Bing, who's moving on to the next verse.

Ty folds his arms and glares out the window. I'm not kidding. Sometimes he can be such a baby.

I don't let him get me down, though. To tell you the truth, I'm excited to be here. I haven't been in the City all that much myself yet, and every time we come in I get excited. Nervous because it's so big and crowded and different and even a little scary sometimes. But excited, too.

Mom reaches over and gives Dad a kiss on the cheek. He laughs. So maybe he's in a good mood now, too, even though we'll be taking cabs and not using the subway.

"'The ox and geese kept time, pa-rum-pum-pum-pum—'" I shout. Wills gets so excited he just starts kicking those fat little legs all over the place.

Everybody, even Ty, laughs.

"Yessir," says Dad, "my son the Rockette."

So we have a pretty good time in the City after all. This is a list of what we do:

1. We go to Rockefeller Center and see the world's biggest outdoor Christmas tree, which has probably about a million strands of lights on it.

2. We buy some pretzels from a street vendor

and eat them. Ty says his is burned, but I like mine just fine.

3. We look at the holiday window displays along Fifth Avenue. The best one is at a department store called Lord & Taylor. It has moving elves doing bike tricks on high wires. Wills squeals when we lift him up to see those elves, and everyone around us laughs. Dad says he can't believe how soft New Yorkers go at the sight of a baby. Especially one who's wearing a little hat with teddy bear ears sent to him by his Aunt Shirley and Aunt Joyce, says Mom.

4. We go to Carnegie Deli to eat. Mom thinks this is really fun, but Dad doesn't. He says he personally isn't charmed by expensive tourist traps where the waiters think they should be tipped extra if they are especially rude to you.

5. We go to the Empire State Building so Mom can see where that old movie star Cary What's-His-Name waited around for his girlfriend all day long. The one who never showed up because her legs got accidentally run over.

6. We buy some more stuff to eat.

Now here comes the part where something major happens.

Mom says it's getting late and that if we want to go to the Museum of Natural History to look at the dinosaur bones, we'd better get moving. Dad sticks out his arm and hops around a little to flag down a taxi because we left our car in a parking terrace not far from Dad's office.

"Stop it, Dad," Ty whispers loudly. "You look like a dork."

"I may be a dork," says Dad as a yellow cab screeches to a stop in front of us, "but I get results, okay?"

I look to see what Ty has to say about this. What I see, instead, is that he has turned into a man with a plan. His eyes are bigger than usual, and he's licking his lips. This can mean only one thing—that he's fixing to jump in the cab first and then lock me out.

Suddenly, Ty swings the cab door open and leaps inside, but I, Sam Evans, am way too fast for my brother.

Well, almost.

I grab the edge of the door before Ty shuts it. Only Ty doesn't see my hand and slams it in the door.

Everything goes dark for a split second, and then pain shoots like flames throughout my whole body so that my toes curl up in my shoes and even my teeth ache. I can't breathe.

Mom screams.

Dad screams.

Ty screams.

Wills screams.

Even the cabbie screams.

I scream, too, because my hand hurts so bad my eyeballs are popping straight out of my face. Ty jumps out of the taxi, his own eyes bigger and wider still. Mom stops screaming and starts wrapping something around my hand. I look down and realize it's one of Wills's diapers. *A diaper*, for Pete's sake.

"He okay?" The cabbie wants to know. "Fingers in door is very bad thing."

"What in the world were you doing?" Dad shouts at Ty. Wills crumples up his face and starts to cry.

So do you want to know what I'm thinking? All in all, this should be a pretty horrible thing. My hand is throbbing, and my family are all screaming at each other. Also, I'm wearing a diaper in public. But here's the weird part—I can't help but notice how *happy* I feel inside. I even say a little prayer inside my head: *Thank you, Heavenly Father, for letting my hand get smashed today.*

No way will I have to play that stupid oboe now.

When Ty slammed that cab door this afternoon, he sure caused a bunch of trouble, and I for one would be totally mad at him if I weren't so totally grateful for being injured. Just for your information, however, here is a list of the trouble that Ty caused:

1. We had to leave Manhattan earlier than expected, so therefore we did not get to see all those old dinosaur bones at the Museum of Natural History.

2. Mom and Dad had another fight in the car on the way home. Dad said my fingers would probably be fine and that I did not need to see a doctor. Mom, on the other hand, said maybe my fingers were broken and that I could be maimed for life and that I should definitely see a doctor.

3. Dad said he broke his fingers playing football in high school and that he knew for sure that my fingers were not broken. Mom said Dad played football back in the Middle Ages and therefore couldn't remember what actual broken fingers looked like.

4. Dad said the doctor's office would be closed on a Saturday afternoon.

5. Mom said fine, pull over to the first instant care place we find in New Jersey.

6. Dad does, but he isn't happy about it, especially when the five of us walk inside and see about a billion people there waiting ahead of us.

As a matter of fact, we've been here for at least an hour. Right now Ty is walking Wills around the waiting room so Wills can see the aquarium for the hundredth time. Wills likes the yellow fish. Ty likes the headless deep-sea diver that somebody forgot to fix. Meanwhile, Dad is grumbling because he can't find any magazines except for back issues of *Highlights*. "I don't want to read about the adventures of Goofus and Gallant," he keeps saying. "I always hated Gallant, anyway. He was such a little brownnoser."

Mom is sitting next to me with her arm draped around my shoulder, trying hard to ignore Dad. I feel nice and warm. "How are you feeling, honey?" she asks.

"Great."

"You know, I was really proud of the way you forgave Ty so quickly."

"Well, I know he didn't mean to hurt me."

Mom gives me a squeeze. "It's kind of funny how you can stay mad at Ty forever when he calls you a name, but when he really hurts you, you behave so maturely. I guess you're just growing up."

I laugh. Weakly. "That would probably be it."

"Sam Evans?" A very short nurse holding a clipboard calls my name.

"Right here," Mom says. The two of us get up

and follow the nurse to a small, clean room where she takes my temperature and checks my blood pressure before getting the lowdown on my hand.

"Yikes!" she says when Mom tells her that I got it slammed in the door of a cab.

"My brother Ty did it," I point out, "but I forgave him."

"Very noble of you," the nurse says. "Dr. Bennett will be here in just a moment. We'll see what she says."

The doctor who shows up is as tall as the nurse is short. She gives Mom and me a big smile that shows a lot of teeth, introduces herself, and then starts to examine my hand.

"Does it hurt when I do this? Or this? What about this?"

It all hurts, actually, but I keep on smiling, I'm just so happy. The only thing that would make me happier is if the doctor tells me I have to get a cast. Then for sure I won't be playing any oboes for Christmas talent shows.

"I honestly don't think anything is broken, Mrs. Evans," Dr. Bennett says after a couple of minutes, "but let's take a couple of X-rays to make sure."

Mom breathes a sigh of relief. "Thank you. I just want to know that he's okay."

It turns out that Dr. Bennett is right. We have

the X-rays taken, and when they come back they show that nothing is broken.

"But I do want you to take it easy, Sam," Dr. Bennett says. "I want you to keep your hand iced and elevated tonight. You can use an ace bandage, too, if that helps."

"Excuse me," I say, "but does this mean I shouldn't play any instruments before Christmas?"

Mom looks at me as if I've suddenly sprouted small red horns out of the sides of my head.

"So you play an instrument?" The doctor acts interested. Why is it every adult person in America is so interested in kids who play musical instruments?

"Well, no, but I've been thinking about—you know—starting lessons and stuff like that."

Mom snorts out loud. Then she coughs to cover it up, but I definitely know a snort when I hear one. Especially when it's one of Mom's snorts.

Dr. Bennett looks at my hand one last time. "I wish all my patients were as pleasant as you are, Sam. You sure are in a good mood for someone who's been hurt."

"Isn't he, though?" Mom says, giving me a curious look.

The doctor tells us how to take care of my hand and then leaves. Mom and I gather up our things.

"Is there something going on you haven't told me about, Sam?" she asks.

A little shiver skips up my back. "No!"

"Okay, then." She slips an arm around me, and we walk out to the waiting room where Wills and Dad are having a fight because Wills wants to take all his clothes off. Frankly, it looks like Wills is winning.

Mom drops a kiss on the top of Dad's head. "No broken fingers for this kid after all."

"Yes!" Dad says as if he's just scored a basket. Then he laughs a little. "It feels good to be right sometimes." He gives me a hug, even though he's clutching Wills's shoes and socks. "Let's go home, everybody."

Home to Shadow! I can hardly wait to cuddle up on the couch with him and tell him all about this day!

Chapter Seven

You would *think* mangling your only right hand would mean you could stay home from church the next day and watch Sports Central Sunday on ESPN with your big black cat curled up on your stomach so that the two of you could find out how the Jazz did. That's what you would think, all right. But no. Mom and Dad say I have to go to church anyway, so here I am sitting in my Primary class listening to Sister Altiere give her lesson.

Sister Altiere, who's probably about sixty or seventy years old, is not like any Primary teacher I ever had in Salt Lake City. For one thing, she wears running shoes with her Sunday dress and also a big floppy straw hat decorated with plastic flowers. For another thing, she's from Jamaica, and when she talks in her soft, low voice, the words go up and down like in a song. Sometimes I have a hard time understanding her, but I always like how she sounds.

Right now, she's telling us that story in the New Testament about the master who gives his servants talents. You remember: the two smart ones take their talents and multiply them so that the guy with three talents ends up with six and the guy with two ends up with four. The stupid servant, however, takes his talent and—duh—buries it straight in the ground.

I've heard this story about a billion times before, but I'm just sitting here totally hypnotized by Sister Altiere's voice.

"And so," Sister Altiere says when she's finished with the parable, "what kind of talents do you have?"

I really cannot believe this. Everywhere I turn these days, somebody is blabbing about talents.

This time around, however, nobody volunteers any information, and it occurs to me that the kids here at church aren't very much like the kids in my school. There's nobody here like Olympia, for instance, who's always raising her hand all over the place, just dying to tell you about that dance she's made up about little flowers coming back to life in the spring.

In fact, as I look around, I realize that most of these kids, whose names I can't even remember from Sunday to Sunday because we all live so far apart, probably don't take a bunch of lessons the way a lot of the kids in my school do. I don't think their families could afford them.

"Does anybody play a musical instrument?" Sister Altiere wants to know.

Everybody shakes their head no, which is a huge relief as far as I'm concerned. Now I won't have to bring up the oboe again.

"What about draw a picture?"

Everybody shakes their head some more.

"Write a book? Star in a movie? Dance a dance?"

We all sit there silently with our mouths sort of hanging open. Sister Altiere looks at us, and then she does the weirdest thing. She clutches her hat with the flowers, throws back her head, and laughs. It's a nice laugh, though. It's not like she's laughing at us because we don't have any talents. Still, I have absolutely no idea why she's laughing.

"Let me tell you about my sister Lily," says Sister Altiere. "My sister Lily, she reads people's hearts. She knows what it is they really think and feel and not just what it is they say. She reads the heart of the rich, important man, and also she reads the heart of the baby sitting on his mother's hip. That is my sister Lily's talent, her gift. And you, my young friends," she points straight at us, "you have your gifts from God, too. I know it."

Sister Altiere's voice doesn't change at all, but there is a tear resting on her cheek, and suddenly I believe her when she says I must have a talent of my own, too.

"You're mighty quiet, Sam," says Mom as we drive home from church. She turns and gives me a concerned smile.

Here's another advantage to smashing your fingers in a taxicab door: grown-ups are really nice to you, even if they do make you go to church. Last night, for example, Mom made a bed for me and Shadow on the couch in front of the TV, and Dad let me have the remote so I got to control what we watched. Even Ty was nice to me last night—he popped me some microwave popcorn. But I could tell this morning when he called me a girl at the breakfast table that he'd gotten over his attack of niceness.

"Are you okay?" Mom wants to know.

"I'm just thinking."

"That's a first," says Ty.

Mom shoots him The Look and then turns back to me. "What are you thinking about?"

If Ty weren't sitting nearby, I might tell her I'm thinking about talents and how talents can be a lot of different things, not just playing an oboe. I

63

might tell her that Sister Altiere promised all of us that we have a talent—a gift from God, she called it—and I want to know what mine is.

Dad is humming "The Little Drummer Boy," Ty is making silly snorting sounds at Wills, and Wills is laughing and pulling Ty's hair with both of his chubby little hands.

"Nothing," I say to Mom. "I'm thinking about nothing."

Chapter Eight

"Sam!" Miss DiMarco gasps when I walk into the classroom Monday morning. "What happened to your poor hand?"

This certainly gets people's attention. All the kids crowd around me to inspect the damage. Everybody except Milo, that is. He just sits at his desk without even looking up, reading an *X-Men* comic book. It's one I haven't read. If Milo and I were fricnds, I'd ask if I could borrow it.

"Well," I say, "we went into the City on Saturday, and my big brother, Tyler, slammed my fingers in the cab door. Cool big brother, huh?"

It's really terrific to see the way everybody, including Miss DiMarco, winces when I explain about my hand.

"That must have hurt like crazy!"

"Did you kill your brother?"

"He ought to be killed for sure!"

"Knowing our Sam, he probably forgave Ty

instantly," Miss DiMarco teases. Still, she actually sounds as if she believes I'm the kind of person who would forgive a big brother for maiming me. Miss DiMarco beams at me in the same way Glinda the Good Witch beams at Dorothy in *The Wizard of Oz*. I start to feel all warm and happy inside.

"I know somebody who got their fingers slammed in a 747 jumbo jet door," says Olympia, but nobody even looks at her. That's because their eyes are all on me and my beautiful, new, black-and-blue hand.

I haven't had this much attention since we moved to New York, and to tell you the truth, it feels great. Just great.

"Oh dear," says Miss DiMarco, looking disappointed. "I just had a thought, Sam. You won't be able to play the oboe in the talent show."

"Even if I had a cast on my leg all the way to the hip, I would still perform my original dance," Olympia says in a loud voice.

"I—I can still try to play if you want me to," I hear myself say.

"Nonsense," says Miss DiMarco. "It's important that those fingers rest so they can heal properly." Then she gives me a smile. "But thanks for the offer."

The bell rings, and I float to my desk, where I

mostly daydream until it's time to go out for morning recess. This is how my daydream goes:

It's the morning of the talent show. The room is packed with parents who are admiring all the decorations our class has made for Christmas. Everybody is admiring my decorations the most. Then Miss DiMarco asks the parents to please take a seat because the talent show is about to begin. After officially welcoming everybody and thanking them for coming, she says, "I want to tell you how disappointed we are that Sam, a truly talented young man, cannot play his oboe for you today because he was involved in a very serious cab injury." Everybody groans when they hear this, and Miss DiMarco nods sadly.

That's when I leap to my feet. "I want to play my oboe, and nobody can stop me!"

"But, Sam," Miss DiMarco protests, "you might ruin your fingers for life."

"That's a risk I'm willing to take," I say. Then I grab my oboe out of my desk, walk up to the front of the room like an injured star power forward limping back out onto the court to help his team, and I play that instrument as it's never been played before . . .

When I go out to recess, kids from different classes come up to me and ask if they can see my fingers. Ty even brings Mason and Julio, as well as those girls Hairy and Scary, over for a look.

By the time recess is almost over, I'm starting to think that maybe New York isn't such a bad place to live after all. I'm in a such a good mood, in fact, I even decide to speak to Milo, who's standing by himself on the edge of the playground, tossing rocks into a monster-sized leafless bush.

"Hi, Milo," I say, joining him.

He doesn't answer but just chucks another stone.

"I said hi." I'm starting to feel a little bugged here. Can't the Mosquito see I'm going out of my way, trying to be nice to him?

"Get outta my face, Sam. We're not friends anymore."

There's the friend thing again. "You keep saying that."

"We *used* to be friends. We used to talk about basketball and stuff."

I can hardly believe my ears. "You used to tell me that the Jazz stink."

"They do. Not that I care anymore." Milo chucks another rock. "Anyway, I hate this stupid school. I hate the way people look down on you if your dad isn't rich."

I'm so surprised I hardly know what to say. "I don't think that's true. My dad isn't rich."

Milo sneers. "Give me a break. Your dad's a lawyer, isn't he?"

The bell rings. The Mosquito tucks his head down and runs inside.

Once we're back in class, I have a continuation of the same daydream, only this time things don't go as well. When I get to the part where I'm limping like a hero with my oboe to the front of the class, Milo stands up and shouts, "The Jazz stink! The Jazz stink! Not that I care anymore!" This upsets me so much I can't play the oboe, even though all the parents are looking up at me, waiting to hear "Frosty the Snowman."

I really hate it when you can't control what happens in your own daydream.

When I get home from school, Mom looks worried.

"Sammy," she says, "I haven't seen Shadow all day."

My stomach turns over. "He was here this morning before I left. I fed him and played with him." I talked to him, too, only I didn't say that part out loud because people think you're weird if you tell them you talk to animals.

"I've looked all through the house and yard, and I haven't seen him," Mom says. "Wills and I even took a long walk and called for him."

"Don't worry. I'll find him," I say, trying to sound calm even though I'm starting to feel a little sick. "I'm going outside to look for Shadow right now."

"Look, Sammy," Mom says taking my arm, "we need to talk about something for a minute."

She makes me sit down in a kitchen chair, and then she pulls up one for herself. "Honey, you know Daddy and I have said all along that Shadow is probably somebody's pet."

"I don't believe it."

Mom takes my face between her hands and kisses me on the forehead. "I just don't want you to be too hurt if Shadow is gone. Okay?"

I swallow hard, give Mom a brief nod, and jump up from my chair. "Anyway, I know Shadow isn't gone," I say as I fly out the kitchen door.

Sometimes grown-ups think they know everything. But they don't.

It's cold outside. The wind is the kind that cuts right through you even when you have a coat on, which I do not. We don't have this kind of wind in Utah. It's getting dark, too, even though it's only about 4:30 in the afternoon. I think all these one-hundred-foot trees standing so close together make it feel darker. I don't really want to go walking through them, to tell you the truth, but I will if I have to.

"Shadow! Here, kitty."

The wind is blowing through the tops of the trees, making them sway and hum. If you were the kind of very stupid person who believed in ghosts, you might think it was ghosts making all the racket.

"Shadow!"

I've been outside only a few minutes, but my hands are starting to feel really frozen. My ears, too. Back home in Utah I never wear a hat and gloves, except when I go skiing. I can't get used to the way you have to put them on every time you go outside here. I rub my hands together and then cup them over my mouth.

"Here, kitty kitty kitty—"

I start walking into the woods, thinking again that it's a very good thing I'm not one of those people who believe in ghosts.

"Shadow!"

Something moves not far from me. It's a small white-tailed deer. She watches me for a second and then leaps off. That's the way it is here. Deer, raccoons, crows, wild turkeys, rabbits, owls, squirrels—

you just never know what kind of animal you're going to see next.

"Meow."

"Shadow?"

Shadow drops out of a tree right in front of me. I practically shoot out of my shoes. Then I start to laugh.

"Come here, boy." I bend down and open my arms. Shadow walks up to me, flicking his big black tail, and lets me pick him up. I look deep into his yellow moon eyes. He stares back at me as if he's trying to tell me something really important—something I can't quite get. Then he just blinks.

When I walk through the kitchen door with old Shadow cradled in my arms, Mom's eyeballs nearly pop out of her head.

"Oh, Sammy, you found him! I thought for sure . . . " She doesn't finish her sentence but reaches instead for Shadow and scratches him underneath his chin. Shadow doesn't mind one little bit.

This feels so good—me and Mom sitting together in a nice warm room with Shadow just purring away.

"You really have a gift, you know, Sam," Mom says.

Now I'm the one who's surprised.

"You have a special talent for making animals feel safe and secure."

"Really? I have a special talent?" I want to hear her say it again.

"Yes," Mom says seriously, "you do. I'm convinced Shadow wouldn't come back here for anybody but you."

Later, Shadow crawls into bed with me.

"Do you think what Mom says is true?" I ask him. "That I have a talent?"

Shadow moves closer to me and purrs.

"I'm glad you're here," I say. "I can't get to sleep."

I think, in fact, I'm the only person in our house who's still awake. Wills conked out a long time ago, and I can hear Ty talking in his sleep in the next room. For a long time the television set in Mom and Dad's room was still on, but even that's quiet now. The house is dark and silent, and even though I know I'm not, I feel all alone.

Except for Shadow.

The moon is very bright tonight, filling my room with milky lights.

I think I can't go to sleep because I keep getting all these pictures in my head—Sister Altiere telling us the story of the talents, everybody at school scoping out my hand except for Milo, Miss DiMarco saying it's too bad I can't play the oboe now, Mom telling me I have a special gift.

I toss and I turn. I turn and I toss. Over and over.

Finally I know what it is I have to do at school tomorrow. Once I realize that, I finally roll over and go to sleep with Shadow still snoozing at my side.

Chapter Nine

I didn't give Mom a chance to ask questions this morning. I waited until she was busy with Wills, and then I said, "I have to be to school early this morning." After that I streaked out the door.

Which is why I'm here before class helping Miss DiMarco set up for the talent show.

"I don't know what I'd do without you, Sam," Miss DiMarco tells me as she slides her desk back against the wall. "Be careful that you don't hurt your hand again."

My stomach is rolling, and my palms are starting to sweat. Miss DiMarco really seems to like me these days. What will she think after I tell her what I have to tell her?

"Does your brother still play the oboe?" I ask, straightening a few chairs. This is the way I plan to bring up the subject of oboes with her.

"Yes. He's a schoolteacher like me, but in his

spare time he plays in a little regional orchestra. Maybe you can do the same thing some day."

"I don't think so," I say truthfully.

Miss DiMarco smiles and gives a little shrug. "That's okay. We don't all have to do the same things."

That's for sure, I think.

"Miss DiMarco? There's something I want to tell you. Actually, I don't *want* to tell you. But I need to."

She looks at me with those huge brown eyes. "What is it, Sam? Are you feeling all right?"

I feel like throwing up, but Miss DiMarco probably doesn't want to hear about that.

"I just have to tell you . . . " Wow, this is a lot harder than I thought it would be. "I just have to tell you that I don't really play the oboe."

Miss DiMarco looks totally and completely surprised.

"I've never even seen one in person before." There. She'll be mad at me for the rest of her life. "Anyway, I thought you ought to know. I'm sorry I lied."

Miss DiMarco speaks slowly, as if she's trying to be careful about what she says next. "It was wrong of you to mislead me, Sam. What made you do it?"

I shrug, hoping like crazy that when I talk I

won't sound as if I'm going to cry. "Because I wanted a talent for the talent show. Everybody else had one. You said yourself you had never had such a talented class before."

"I see." She reaches to the floor and picks up a stray scrap of paper, which she starts to fold and unfold. "Why did you decide to tell me all this, Sam? I probably would have never known the truth."

I think back to last night with Shadow curled up beside me when I decided to let Miss DiMarco know that I don't really play the oboe. "Because I guess I realized I have a talent after all. Just not the kind you can see."

"Just not the kind you can see," she repeats my words to herself as if I'm not even there.

Suddenly a couple of kids burst through the classroom door. One of them has a violin case, and the other is carrying a huge canvas. "We're ready for the talent show!" they say.

Everybody's parents start to come around 9:30. They smile and say hello to each other and to us and to Miss DiMarco, too. One lady who walks in has a huge diamond ring on her finger, as well as a live little dog tucked underneath her arm. Right away you just know she's Olympia's mother. The rest of the parents look pretty normal—moms in nice slacks and dads in suits, except for one guy who has on jeans, work boots, and an old sweatshirt. He seems nice, but he does look kind of out of place.

At 9:40, just a few minutes before the talent show is supposed to start, I get a little surprise. Mom and Wills show up. Mom gives me a little wave, and Wills burps so that all the kids start to laugh.

So how did *they* know about the talent show? I'm pretty sure I threw away everything from the school that mentioned it.

Miss DiMarco stands up in front of the class and gives one of her primo smiles. "I'd like to welcome you all to the Tuxedo Park School Sixth-Grade Holiday Talent Show. These students have worked long and hard to prepare for this special event, and I want them to know how truly proud of them I am."

The kids all smile. The parents all clap.

"Before we turn the time over to this room full of stars"—everybody chuckles—"I just want to say something. I love teaching your children, and I especially love the things they teach me. Just this morning, for example, I was reminded by one of them that there are all kinds of talents, not just the ones we will enjoy this morning. I want to thank that student for teaching me something important that I had forgotten."

Oh my gosh! She's talking about me. Miss DiMarco is really talking about *me!* I can't believe my ears! Mom, who's sitting on the front row, looks back at me and smiles. Suddenly I realize that Miss DiMarco called Mom to make sure she'd be here.

Wow.

The show starts, and the truth is that I have a lot of fun watching everybody. Angela plays "Jingle Bells" on the flute. Thomas plays "Jingle Bells" on the violin. Alexander plays "Jingle Bells" on the piano. Elizabeth sings. Michael sings. Winston shows us a sculpture. Olivia shows us a picture. It's all great stuff.

I even like Olympia's dance about the little flower who comes back to life in the spring, mostly because her tutu accidentally slips off in the middle of her performance. She screams so loud her mother's little dog starts to bark. I love it. Barking dogs at school.

I'll tell you whose performance I like the best, though—Milo's.

He gets up in front of us and announces, "I'm going to recite a poem called 'Stopping by Woods on a Snowy Evening,' by Robert Frost." Then he clears his throat and starts in a strong, loud voice:

> *Whose woods these are I think I know.*
> *His house is in the village, though;*
> *He will not see me stopping here*
> *To watch his woods fill up with snow.*
>
> *My little horse must think it queer*
> *To stop without a farmhouse near*
> *Between the woods and frozen lake*
> *The darkest evening of the year.*
>
> *He gives his harness bells a shake*
> *To ask if there is some mistake.*
> *The only other sound's the sweep*
> *Of easy wind and downy flake.*
>
> *The woods are lovely, dark and deep,*
> *But I have promises to keep,*
> *And miles to go before I sleep,*
> *And miles to go before I sleep.*

I can almost see the poem happen as Milo says the words because he says them with so much feeling, and when I look outside the window, I wish with all my heart that the bare branches were covered with snow.

After the program, we serve our parents red punch and cookies shaped like stars and Christmas trees. I notice that Milo serves the man in jeans who reaches up and ruffles Milo's hair just as Dad does to me sometimes. I hate it when he does that because it messes my hair up and makes me feel like I'm Wills's age. But I sort of like it, too. Does that make any sense? I wonder if Milo feels the same way.

When I sit down by Mom she winks at me and says, "Thanks a lot for letting me know about the talent show."

"Miss DiMarco called you this morning, right?"

Mom nods. Then she takes my hand and squeezes it. "I'm proud of you, Sam."

Later that day when I see Milo sitting at the lunch table, I stop a minute to tell him I liked that poem he memorized.

"What else could I do?" he grumbles into his cottage-fried potatoes. "I don't have a real talent."

"You're smart," I point out. "You know all about hysterical numbers and stuff."

"Big deal. And they're not hysterical numbers, for your information. They're irrational numbers."

"Whatever," I shrug.

Milo shovels some more potatoes into his mouth.

"Anyway," I say, before moving on, "I liked the

poem about the snow. I wish there were snow out-side right now."

As I leave, Milo calls after me, "Hey, Sam, you know something? The Jazz stink."

Okay. I want to make something perfectly clear here. This is *not* going to be one of those stories where Milo and I suddenly discover we have a whole bunch of things in common. We don't start calling girls on the telephone together to see what they think about us. We don't start playing Sega or air hockey. We don't start watching basketball games on TV because Milo suddenly sees the light and becomes converted to the Jazz. We definitely don't become best friends, because the truth is I find him extremely annoying.

It's just that for some reason I don't mind the way he annoys me as much anymore.

Chapter Ten

Yes!

School's out, and in three more days it will be Christmas.

Yes!

We'll wrap presents and listen to Christmas music and drink lots of hot chocolate. We'll wait for the mailman every day to see what he brings. We'll take Wills to the mall in Nanuet and let him sit on Santa's lap, and if we're really lucky, maybe he'll pull off Santa's beard.

Yesohyesohyes!

Hillary and her roommate Sybill, who has purple hair and a pierced nose, drove down from Hamilton, New York, last night, and Aunt Shirley and Aunt Joyce are flying into Stewart International today. They'll have homemade popcorn balls and a big bag full of candy—Smarties and caramels and swedish fish—tucked in their suitcases. When they get here they'll set up the Monopoly board and

we'll play and play until we get sick of Monopoly
and want to play Clue instead. I'm so happy they're
coming I don't even mind that they'll be using my
bedroom, which means I have to sleep in a sleeping bag on Ty's floor. Mom's in my room now,
changing sheets and getting everything ready.

Right now I'm in the kitchen with Hillary and
Sybill, eating bagels and cream cheese.

"This is a great house, Sam," says Hillary. She's
got Wills in her lap, and he's trying to steal her
food.

"It's okay."

"Homesick still?" She gives me a sympathetic
look.

I shrug. "A little, I guess."

"The first few months I was here I was so homesick I wanted to die," Hillary says.

"It's true," Sybill chimes in. "Sometimes we
thought she must have died during the night
because we couldn't get her out of bed in the
morning to go to class."

"It's a wonder I didn't totally flunk out," Hillary
smiles. "I just missed home so much. I missed my
family and friends. I missed stuff about Salt Lake,
too. I missed the way rain cooled everything down
and made the air smell like sagebrush instead
of turning it all thick and muggy. I missed the sun

setting over the lake. I missed getting Big H hamburgers at Hires."

I laugh. We used to go to Hires, too.

"I missed the familiar faces on the ten o'clock news. I missed the wide streets and the aspen turning yellow in September," Hillary goes on.

"And seeing Jazz games on TV," I add.

"Exactly. But I feel better now. Plus you gotta admit there are things here we can't get at home. Like decent bagels, for instance," she says as she pops a piece of an egg bagel into her mouth.

"Things have gotten a little better here since Shadow showed up." I can't believe I actually say this, but when I hear the words I realize they're true.

"Who's Shadow?" Sybill asks.

"Our cat. He's really huge."

"A big fat sumo cat!" says Sybill. "I love sumo cats! Where is he?"

"He's probably hiding because he's kind of shy, but I can find him," I say. "I'll be right back."

First I look in his favorite spot—my bedroom. "Is Shadow in here?" I ask Mom, who's spreading a newly cleaned comforter across my bed.

"I haven't seen him, Sam."

So I check his second favorite spot—the couch in the living room.

He isn't there.

Time to look for Shadow in his third favorite spot—Wills's crib. Mom goes totally nuts when she finds Shadow in there. It doesn't stop him from crawling in though. Shadow, however, is not in Wills's crib.

"No sumo cat?" says Sybill when I join her and Hillary and Wills in the kitchen.

"He's probably outside. I'll go find him."

"That's okay. I'll just meet him later," says Sybill, but I pull on my coat anyway and run out the kitchen door.

"Shadow!"

I half expect Shadow to emerge out of a bush or drop on all fours from a tree, but he doesn't.

Still, I'm not too worried. Shadow's probably off chasing mice somewhere.

Dad walks out of the house and calls to me, "Hey, Sammy, do you want to drive to the airport with me to pick up Aunt Shirley and Aunt Joyce?"

"Sure!"

When we get back I bet Shadow will be curled up on my pillow, wondering where in the world I've been.

"Oh my! What a beautiful house!" Aunt Shirley says when we pull into our driveway.

"Isn't it just?" says Aunt Joyce. "I think it's the most beautiful house I've ever seen."

Dad and I both laugh. The two of them have been saying stuff like this all the way home from the airport. Aunt Shirley would say isn't that a beautiful tree and Aunt Joyce would say isn't it just? I think it's the most beautiful tree I've ever seen. Dad always says what makes Aunt Shirley and Aunt Joyce so much fun to be around is that they like to be happy.

"Wait until you see Wills," Dad says as he gets out of the car and opens the door for the aunts. "You won't believe how huge he is."

"I'll just bet he's smart, too," says Aunt Shirley.

"The smartest baby in New York, no doubt," says Aunt Joyce.

"Handsome as well," says Aunt Shirley.

"Naturally," says Aunt Joyce. "All our people are handsome."

"We have a new cat, too," I say as I help Dad lift suitcases out of the trunk.

"A cat?" says Aunt Shirley. "I love cats."

"He's black," I say. "Like our old cat Shadow. In fact, this cat's name is Shadow, too."

"Black cats are my favorite," says Aunt Joyce. "If I had a cat, I would most definitely want him to be black."

"I don't think we'll be getting a black cat any-time soon, however, Sam," says Aunt Shirley. "Our Petie wouldn't like it."

Petie is the parakeet who lives with Aunt Shirley and Aunt Joyce. He does tricks, like hanging upside down from his swing and pulling a little plastic cart around on top of the dining room table.

Everybody is happy to see everybody when we go inside. Aunt Shirley and Aunt Joyce hug Mom and Ty and Wills. They hug Hillary, and they even hug Sybill after checking out her nose ring and purple hair. Then Aunt Shirley and Aunt Joyce open up one of their suitcases. It's stuffed with homemade popcorn balls.

"Of course we brought the usual caramel pop-corn balls," says Aunt Shirley, "but we've been doing a little experimenting recently. See these red and green popcorn balls?"

Everyone nods.

"Jell-O," says Aunt Shirley proudly.

"They're good, too," says Aunt Joyce. "Almost as good as the caramel."

"But not quite," says Aunt Shirley.

"No, not quite," agrees Aunt Joyce.

"Although I like the marshmallows we put in them," says Aunt Joyce.

"Oh yes, the marshmallows are a nice touch,"

agrees Aunt Joyce. She reaches in the suitcases, grabs a few popcorn balls, and tosses them at us as if she were a cheerleader throwing out miniature footballs to the crowd at half-time

"Do you want to see our cat?" I finally think to ask as I finish off one of the Jell-O popcorn balls.

"Of course we do," says Aunt Shirley.

So I walk through the house calling for Shadow to come, only he doesn't. And when I look for him outside, I still can't find him.

"I'm sure he's fine," Dad says when I tell him I'm worried about Shadow. "Maybe he's out doing a little Christmas shopping. Ha! Ha!" When Dad sees I'm not laughing, he slips his arm around my shoulders and gives me a squeeze. "Cheer up, Sam. It's almost Christmas. Everything's going to be just fine."

I don't know. I just hope he's right.

Chapter Eleven

It's Christmas Eve.

Mom likes to say this is the most magical day of the whole year because everything around you is a promise. Take a gift sitting under the Christmas tree, she says. That's a promise of having your heart's desire fulfilled. Or take the warm, quiet feeling you get when you sing "Silent Night" in church. That's a promise of peace.

I'm not sure I know what she means by all that stuff, to tell you the truth. I just like Christmas Eve because it's so exciting. You wake up with this little tickle in your stomach that just keeps getting bigger and bigger. Every time you look at your Christmas tree with the lights turned on or smell something good baking in the kitchen, the tickle grows until you're so excited you can't even think or sit still.

Only today I don't feel that way because Shadow

is still gone. And this time I think he's gone for good.

I spent yesterday looking for him. Even though there's still no snow, it was freezing cold, but I stayed outside most of the day just walking and calling, calling and walking. Ty helped, too, for part of the time. So did Dad and Mom. Even Aunt Shirley joined me once because she said she knows how it feels to lose a pet you love. When she was a little girl she had a white rabbit named Snowball who got out of his cage in the middle of the night and scampered away.

"Did you ever find him?" I asked.

"Well, no," said Aunt Shirley.

That wasn't exactly the kind of story I wanted to hear.

So now it's Christmas Eve, and Shadow is still missing. I'm just sitting by the living room window, looking into the woods across the street, even though it's really too dark to see anything.

"Come join us, Sammy," says Aunt Joyce. She and Aunt Shirley and Ty and Hillary and Sybill are playing Scrabble. The only time Aunt Shirley and Aunt Joyce fight is when they play Scrabble because they always think the other one is cheating. This is how Aunt Shirley and Aunt Joyce fight: one of them says to the other one that she doesn't really have naturally curly hair but has a permanent wave every six months instead. I'm not kidding. But tonight it looks like they're getting along just fine.

"Yeah, Sam, come on," Ty urges. It's almost weird how nice he's being to me, which means I'll be forced to revise my list about Big Brothers.

"No thanks," I say.

A fire is roaring in the fireplace, Mom's serving hot chocolate to everyone, Wills is trying to open up all the presents, and the radio is playing "Rudolph the Red-Nosed Reindeer"—it certainly *looks* like Christmas at our house.

It just doesn't feel like Christmas.

I wonder how cold it is outside. Where is Shadow? Is he hungry? Is he scared?

Dad enters the living room, a huge black Bible tucked under his arm. His great-grandfather used to own it, so it's really old and fragile. The binding is starting to crack and peel. During the rest of the year Dad keeps this Bible in a safe place, but on Christmas Eve, ever since I can remember, he pulls it out and reads to us about that long ago night when Jesus was born.

"Gather around, one and all," says Dad. "Time to hear the best story ever."

He sits down in the rocking chair, and everyone else fills up the couch and the rest of the chairs, including the one Shadow likes to sit on. I finally pull myself away from the window and sit on the hearth next to the crackling flames.

Dad opens the big Bible and carefully turns the pages. Then he clears his throat and begins to read in a big booming voice: "And it came to pass in those days, that there went out a decree from Caesar Augustus, that all the world should be taxed."

I can see it all in my head—Joseph lifting Mary onto the donkey, the donkey carrying her through the streets of Bethlehem, Joseph going from door to door looking for a place to stay.

Suddenly it all seems so sad—people far away from home, people not being able to find a place to stay. I jump up and run outside. I hear Ty call my name, but Mom tells him to shush.

I'm all alone, so do you know what I do next? I cry. I hate it when I cry, but that's what I do. I sit down on the freezing cold front porch and let loose all the hot tears that have been building up. They just slide down my face, and I don't do anything at all to stop them.

I just cry and cry like some huge, embarrassing baby.

After a little while I hear the door behind me

open. It's Dad. He steps out onto the porch and hands me my coat, plus a hat and some gloves.

"We finished the story without you, Sammy," he says. "I hope you don't mind."

"That's okay. I know how it ends."

"May I join you for a minute?"

"That's okay, too."

Dad sits next to me on the top stair.

He points over our shoulders at the living room window. It looks like a frame for the picture inside—Mom, Ty, Wills, Aunt Shirley, Aunt Joyce, Hillary, and Sybill all enjoying Christmas Eve.

"I feel like we're running an inn!" he laughs.

"Only Mom wouldn't turn anybody away," I say.

Dad looks at me closely. "You're right," he says. "She wouldn't."

We sit together for a while without talking, just looking together at the woods across the street. Pretty soon the moon starts to rise over the tops of the trees. It's big and white, almost full. Suddenly we see three deer standing in the trees, staring back at us. In the moonlight, their eyes look silver.

"I wonder if they know it's Christmas," I say.

"There's a legend about animals at Christmastime," Dad tells me. "The legend goes that at midnight animals everywhere are given the gift of speech."

"Really?" I like this legend a lot. "I wonder what those deer would say to us. I wonder what rabbits would say and raccoons and crows, too."

Dad smiles and shrugs. Then he puts his arm across my shoulder. "I think I know what a certain black cat would say."

I swallow hard, and Dad goes on. "I think he would tell you that he was just passing through on his way to somewhere else but that he liked you so much he stayed longer than he had planned to. I think he would say thank you for giving him good food to eat and a warm bed to sleep on. I think he would say thank you for being the kind of innkeeper that doesn't turn away cats."

I feel like laughing and crying at the same time.

"Is that what you think Shadow would say tonight?"

"Yes," says Dad, "that's most definitely what I think Shadow would say tonight."

The deer across the street take one last look at us and then turn and walk as slowly as kings into the trees until they disappear, also on their way to someplace else.

"It's getting really cold out here, Sammy. Let's go in now."

"You go," I say. "I'll come in soon."

"Promise?"

"I promise."

So Dad leaves me here on the porch, and I think just a minute longer—think and remember. I remember the first time I saw Shadow in the woods and the time Ty tried to call him but scared him off. I think about the Saturday morning Dad was making pancakes and how I slipped outside and found Shadow for myself. I think about the way Shadow used to curl up next to me in bed and purr. And finally I remember the time I thought Shadow was trying to tell me something only I didn't understand.

Then I say out loud, only not so loud I might sound crazy to someone just passing by, "Good-bye, Shadow. Have a happy life."

"Wake up, Sammy! Wake up!" Mom's shaking me.

"Is it morning already?" I feel as if I've just gone to sleep.

"No, but there's something I want you to see. Here." She hands me my coat and a pair of boots. "Just put these on over your pajamas."

I roll out of my sleeping bag and fumble around for a minute, trying to get dressed. Then I follow Mom down the stairs and—here's the weird part—out the front door even though it's the middle of the night.

"DUCK, SAM!" Ty sends something whizzing past my ear. It takes me a minute to realize it's a snowball.

A SNOWBALL!

MY BROTHER JUST THREW A SNOWBALL AT ME HERE IN NEW YORK!

Everywhere I look there's snow—snow on the ground, on the rocks, on the branches of trees, on the fence, on the mailbox, on top of our house. It's falling across the face of the moon. It's falling everywhere, like lacy curtains from the sky.

"Yes!" I cry.

Ty throws a snowball at Dad, who throws one back at him. Hillary and Sybill laugh. Aunt Shirley and Aunt Joyce ask if anyone wants to play fox and geese. Somewhere in the distance, church bells ring.

Mom walks up behind me, slides her arm around my shoulders, and whispers, "Merry Christmas, Sam Evans. How do you like this snow Dad and I arranged for you?"

Then, lifting her arms up as if she's going to catch the snow falling straight from the sky, she roars out a laugh.

And so do I.

About the Author

Ann Edwards Cannon is an award-winning writer who lives with her husband, Ken, and their five sons in Salt Lake City, Utah. She has written a number of books for young readers, including *Amazing Gracie, The Shadow Brothers, I Know What You Do When I Go to School,* and *Great-Granny Rose and the Family Christmas Tree.*

Sam's Gift was inspired by experiences the Cannon family shared when they lived in a wonderful old stone house surrounded by woods in New York state.